For my granddaughter,
Anna Penelope Rose
P.L.

PUFFIN BOOKS

Published by the Penguin Group
Penguin Books Ltd, 27 Wrights Lane, London W8 5TZ, England
Penguin Putnam Inc., 375 Hudson Street, New York, New York 10014, USA
Penguin Books Australia Ltd, Ringwood, Victoria, Australia
Penguin Books Canada Ltd, 10 Alcorn Avenue, Toronto, Ontario, Canada M4V 3B2
Penguin Books (NZ) Ltd, Private Bag 102902, NSMC, Auckland, New Zealand

On the world wide web at: www.penguin.com

Penguin Books Ltd, Registered Offices: Harmondsworth, Middlesex, England

First published by Viking 1998
Published in Puffin Books 1999
10 9 8 7 6 5 4 3 2 1

Text copyright © Penelope Lively, 1998
Illustrations copyright © Jan Ormerod, 1998
All rights reserved

The moral right of the author and illustrator has been asserted

Made and printed in Italy by Printer Trento srl

British Library Cataloguing in Publication Data
A CIP catalogue record for this book is available from the British Library

ISBN 0–140–55966–3

ONE · TWO · THREE
JUMP!

Penelope Lively
Illustrated by Jan Ormerod

PUFFIN BOOKS

The dragonfly had eyes that could see front,
back and sideways.

The dragonfly could see everything at once.
She could see all of the garden.

The frog lived between two stones.
I want to be somewhere else, thought the frog.
I want to see things. I want to jump.

Let's go. One, two, three . . .

...jump!

The frog jumped as far as he could go.

"Excuse me," said a voice.
The frog looked up and saw the dragonfly.
"The garden path is not a good place for a
young frog to be," said the dragonfly.

"Why?" said the frog. "It's exciting."
"Don't ask questions," said the dragonfly.
"Just jump – quick!
One, two, three . . .

So the frog jumped . . . just in time.

The frog sat under a big leaf and looked around.
"It's good here," he said.
"There are things that wave and things
that wobble and mysterious shadows."

"Exactly," said the dragonfly. "That's the trouble.
Quick! One, two, three . . .

...¡ump!,,

The frog jumped . . . just in time.

The frog jumped out on to the lawn
– and there was the dragonfly.
"You again!" said the frog. "Now listen –
I'm as green as the grass and no one can see me.
This is where I'm going to stay."

"I wouldn't do that," said the dragonfly.

"I don't have to do what you tell me," said the frog.

"Indeed you don't," said the dragonfly.

"But if you've got any sense at all, jump!

Quick! One, two, three . . .

...jump!"

So the frog jumped . . . just in time!

He went up and up and
then he went down and down
until he dropped, plop . . .

. . . into the bottom of a deep hole.
"This time I'm stopping where I am,"
said the frog. "This hole will do fine.
I have a stone to get underneath if I feel like it,
and this worm to talk to if I need a friend.
And when I want to go jumping – well, I can."

"If I were you I'd jump right now,"
said the dragonfly. "Quick!"

"I'M NOT GOING TO,"
said the frog.

And then he saw what the dragonfly could see.

He jumped the furthest he had ever jumped before . . .

. . . and landed with a **splash!** in the most wonderful place he could ever have imagined. "Where's this?" cried the frog.

"This is the pond," said the dragonfly.
"And here's the right place for a young frog to be.
Have fun!"

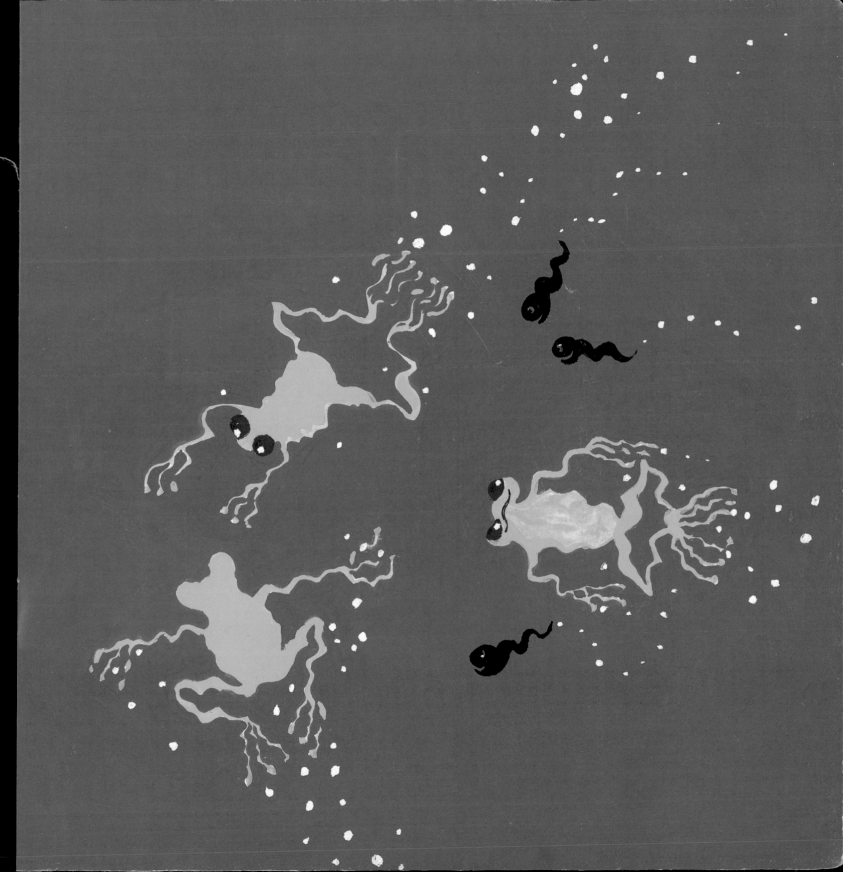